A Curious Christmas

Erica Elemes

Illustrated by Rebecca Koerner

Copyright © 2016 by Erica Elemes. 733421

ISBN: Softcover   978-1-5144-5139-7
        EBook   978-1-5245-4273-3

All rights reserved. No part of this book may be reproduced or transmitted in any form or by any means, electronic or mechanical, including photocopying, recording, or by any information storage and retrieval system, without permission in writing from the copyright owner.

This is a work of fiction. Names, characters, places and incidents either are the product of the author's imagination or are used fictitiously, and any resemblance to any actual persons, living or dead, events, or locales is entirely coincidental.

Print information available on the last page.

Rev. date: 08/31/2016

To order additional copies of this book, contact:
Xlibris
1-888-795-4274
www.Xlibris.com
Orders@Xlibris.com

It was almost Christmas. Everyone at the North Pole was hustling about.

The elves in the workshop were busy making toys and wrapping presents.

In the kitchen, Mrs. Claus was baking cookies and other Christmas delights.

Santa was checking The Naughty and Nice List for the second time.

Watching all the excitement was a boy elf named Ginger Cookie. He was bursting with curiosity about how Santa would deliver all those presents in just one night. He couldn't wait for Christmas Eve.

Christmas Eve finally arrived and the elves helped Santa ready the sleigh. When the presents were loaded and the reindeer geared up, Mrs. Claus asked, "Santa, are you all set?"

"You bet your sprinkles I am!" Santa replied.

After a kiss and a hug, Santa called to his Reindeer. On Dasher! On Dancer! On Prancer and Vixen! And into the sky they rose.

Little did Santa know, there were more than presents in his sleigh. Ginger was hiding under the bag of toys!

The sleigh flew through the midnight sky, over the mountains, and around the moon. As Ginger looked over the edge of the sleigh, a sleepy town came into sight.

Carefully, Santa landed his team of reindeer on the first housetop. Jumping out of the sleigh, he picked up his sack and walked to the chimney.

With the wave of his hand and a nod of his head, the chimney grew bigger and Santa climbed down. As quick as a wink, the chimney shrunk back.

Gingers eyes grew wide. "So that's how Santa fits in the chimney!" Ginger whispered to himself. A minute later, Santa returned to the roof, climbed in the sleigh and took off to the next house.

House after house, Ginger watched as Santa used his magic to open the chimneys. Filled with curiosity about what was happening down below, Ginger decided to follow Santa into the next house. After they landed, Ginger ever so carefully tip-toed behind Santa. As soon as Santa went down the chimney, Ginger jumped to follow.

Everything went dark except for a bright light shining warmly. Ginger tried to move to his left, then to his right. "Oh no!" Ginger thought, "I'm stuck in the Chimney!"

And stuck he was! Half way in and half way out, he was quite the sight. Even the reindeer were laughing!

"I have to get out before Santa comes back!" Ginger thought to himself.

He whistled to the reindeer to help pull him out, but the chimney was too small and too tight.

Suddenly, he felt a tickle, a tingle, and a wiggle. The chimney grew bigger and Santa came up, knocking Ginger loose. "My goodness! What are you doing here?" Santa exclaimed.

"Oh Santa," Ginger cried, "I'm sorry! I just wanted to see how you deliver all the presents, so I hid under the bag of toys. I know what I did was wrong. Can you ever forgive me?"

Santa saw that Ginger felt bad about sneaking onto the sleigh. As Ginger had learned his lesson, Santa replied, "Of course I forgive you! Since it is Christmas, how would you like to help me deliver the rest of these presents?"

"Oh YES! I would!" Ginger exclaimed.

Santa and Ginger hopped into the sleigh and flew to the next house. "Now hold my hand, young elf, as we go down, and you won't get stuck," Santa told Ginger as they approached the chimney. Ginger held Santa's hand as they jumped down the chimney.

The two climbed out on to the hearth to find a room lit only by a Christmas tree. Stepping past milk and cookies left out for expected visitors, Santa reached inside his coat for his list. "Ah!" Santa exclaimed, "This is Billy and Susie Turner's house. Ginger, reach into my bag for their presents!"

Ginger looked into Santa's bag and a new bicycle for Billy and a dollhouse for Susie appeared. He looked at Santa in awe and asked "How?" "Why Christmas Magic of course!" exclaimed Santa as he set the presents below the tree. Then the two went back up the chimney and took flight towards the next house.

Santa and Ginger continued until a present had been delivered to every name on Santa's list. As they flew back to the North Pole, Ginger thought about the amazing night he had experienced, and was sad that it was at an end. Seeing that Ginger looked disappointed, Santa said, "Cheer up, Ginger! Though Christmas may be over, remember the most magical part of Christmas is that there will be another one next year!" Hearing this, Ginger smiled happily to himself.

Ginger learned a valuable lesson that night, and to this day it remains a Christmas he will never forget.

Symmetrical Elf Feet

After reading <u>A Curious Christmas</u> about Ginger Cookie and his Christmas Eve adventure, make your very own elf who gets stuck in the chimney!

Materials:
- 1– Large piece of black construction paper (12″ x18″)
- 1- chimney colored medium sized construction paper (9″ x 12″)
- 2-medium sized piece of construction paper (9″ x 12″) in colors of your choice
- Several small pieces of construction paper in assorted colors
- Glue
- Scissors
- Glitter for snow (optional)

Symmetry: Being the same on both sides.
Examples of Symmetry: Hearts, Butterflies, the letter H

Before you begin:
Discuss Symmetry-being the same on both sides. Some **examples of Symmetry are** Hearts, Butterflies, the letter H. To make Symmetrical shapes we can fold a paper in half and cut two shapes at the same time. Once cut you have to flip one over to make it be the mirror image.

Step One:
To make the legs take the medium construction paper (color of your choice) and fold it in half the long way

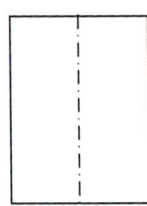

Step Two:
Draw the legs of the elf from the top of the paper to the bottom. Leg should be a few inches thick, but do not draw the feet! Then cut out legs from paper.

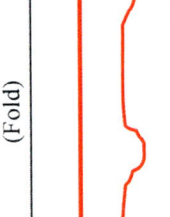
(Fold)

Step Three:
Glue legs to the bottom of the large black paper leaving space for the elf shoes.

Step four: (elf shoes)

Take another construction paper piece (color of your choice) and fold it in half. Draw one elf shoe. Cut out and flip one of the shoes to create the mirror image or symmetry.

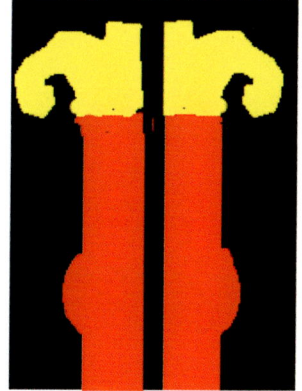

Step five:

Decorate elf legs and feet as you wish using symmetrical designs

Step Six:

Carefully cut around elf feet to create a black border all the way around.

Step Seven: (the chimney)

Using the chimney paper fold paper in half. Cut out a rectangle from the side that is NOT folded to create a "T" shape.

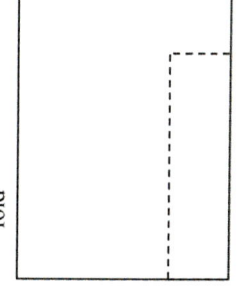

fold

Step Eight:

Unfold and decorate chimney as desired. Some options are to cut out brick shapes from pieces of paper and glue on top, Draw bricks with a marker. Use liquid glue to add glitter to create a snow effect on the chimney.

Step Nine:

Glue or tape elf feet to back of chimney

Step Ten:

Enjoy!

ABOUT THE BOOK AND THE CREATORS

A Curious Christmas was written as a fun project that Erica Elemes and Rebecca Koerner came together on as a great example of project based learning. Mrs. Elemes was teaching art at St. Joseph's School in Moorhead, Minnesota to grades K–8. The book started as just a fun idea for a second grade art project Mrs. Elemes was teaching. From there, the idea blossomed. Mrs. Elemes was originally going to also be the illustrator, but Rebecca was suggested by another teacher at St. Joe's, Mrs. Jeanne Lindquist.

After Mrs. Elemes was done writing the story, Rebecca worked long and hard on every drawing. She brainstormed ideas with Mrs. Elemes about what she was picturing for them, and throughout many months they

worked on it. Starting off with traditional work, she ended up transferring all of them digitally to reline and recolor every picture. The illustrations were made with love and hard work and make the book an amazing experience for everyone who reads it.

Erica Elemes, originally from Medora, North Dakota now resides in New Richmond, Wisconsin with her husband Dan and their dog Charlie. She continues to teach and share her love of art.

Her student, Rebecca Koerner, was in eight grade at St. Joseph's at the time the book was created. She spends lots of her time outside of school drawing whenever she can and has been doing lots of fun drawing assignments with her teacher Mrs. Elemes.

Edwards Brothers Malloy
Thorofare, NJ USA
November 11, 2016